D0605510

FRED Forgets

JARVIS

HARPER
An Imprint of HarperCollins*Publishers*

Fred Forgets

For information address HarperCollins Children's Books, a division of HarperCollins Publishers, 195 Broadway, New York, NY 10007.
www.harpercollinschildrens.com

ISBN 978-0-06-234916-3 (trade bdg.)

The artist used pencil, paint, and chalk to create the digital illustrations for this book.
Typography by Jeanne L. Hogle
16 17 18 19 20 SCP 10 9 8 7 6 5 4 3 2 1
❖

FOR MUM & DAD

This is Fred.
He was just about to do something . . .

but he has forgotten what it is.

"Um, I forgot what I was doing . . . ?"

"Oh, um, I think you said you were going to ride a unicycle upside down," said Monkey.

"Ah, yes . . . that's right. I remember now."

WOBBLE
WOBBLE

HEE-
HEE

"Wait. . . . My legs are tired!

What am I doing?"

"Hee-hee. I don't know. . . . You must be thirsty. I think you said you were going to drink swamp water."

"Ah, yes! . . . I AM thirsty. I remember that now."

SLURP
GLUG

HEE-
HEE

"Wait. . . . Yuck! This is disgusting!
What am I doing?"

"Hee-hee. I don't know. That swamp was pretty disgusting! So—you said you were going to go for a swim in the sea . . . with sharks."

"I did? Okay, um . . . I guess I remember that now. Where are my goggles?"

SPLISH SPLOSH

HEE-
HEE-

"Wait. . . . This is scary! I'm not a shark, I'm an elephant!

What am I doing swimming with sharks??"

"Hee-hee. I don't know! You ARE an elephant. A big and strong elephant . . . and I think you said you're about to wrestle a rhino."

"I am? Of course I am. I remember that now.

I hope I win!"

HEE-HEE
ROUND ONE
FRED

GRRR
THE BIG R

FRE
THE BIG R

"Wait. . . . This isn't fun. Ouch!

What am I doing?"

"Hee-hee. I don't know! You need something to cheer you up. . . . I think you were about to put on a nice dress and sing a happy song. Does that sound right?"

"Ah, yes . . . of course I was. I remember now."

"Happy, happy, la la,
I can't remember the words,
doo dee doo."
HEE-HEE

"Wait. . . . Why am I wearing a dress and
why are my friends laughing at me?
What am I doing?"

"Hee–hee. I don't know . . . but you're my friend too! And you were going to peel me a million bananas."

"Ah, yes. . . . I am a good friend. I remember now."

"Four hundred and thirty-two!
Four hundred and thirty-three!
Four-hundred and thirty-four!"

"Wait! . . . I just remembered what I was supposed to do."
"You do?"

"Yes. Hee-hee."

NO ELEPHANTS OR MONKEYS WERE HARMED IN THE MAKING OF THIS BOOK
FRED